WOODY

by Nicholas Heller

Greenwillow Books, New York

Watercolor paints and a black pen line were used for the full-color art. The text type is Cooper Lt. BT.

Printed in Singapore by Tien Wah Press

First Edition   10 9 8 7 6 5 4 3 2 1

LIBRARY OF CONGRESS CATALOGING-IN-PUBLICATION DATA
Heller, Nicholas.
Woody / by Nicholas Heller.
        p.   cm.
Summary: Woody the pig is bored, until he spends an afternoon wishing himself into various adventurous situations.
ISBN 0-688-12804-1 (trade).   ISBN 0-688-12805-X (lib. bdg.)
[1. Pigs—Fiction.   2. Wishes—Fiction.]   I. Title.
PZ7.H37426Wo   1994   [E]—dc20
93-13247   CIP   AC

"I'm bored," Woody said.

"Then go find something to do outside," suggested his mother. "It's a fine-looking afternoon."

Woody went out and sat down in the middle of a
field. "I wish I were doing something really exciting,"
he muttered, idly plucking a dandelion.
"Humph," he said, and puffed as hard as he could.

"Oh, my goodness. What's happening?" cried
Woody as he found himself plummeting headfirst
through the air. "Yaaaa!"

A parachute billowed open above him, slowing
his fall. "Oh, I see!" said Woody.

Woody landed back in the field with a thump,
and immediately plucked another dandelion.
"That was exciting! Now," he said, "I wish I were a
football player." And he puffed with all his might.

WHOOOSH!
Woody was in a huge stadium. Crowds were
cheering, and the ball was headed his way.
He leaped to catch it.

I'm going to make a touchdown! thought
Woody as he sprinted up the field at full speed.

"Uh, oh!"

"I wish," gasped Woody from the bottom of the
pile, "I were a knight in armor!" And he blew
on a handy dandelion.

"That's better," said Woody. The stadium had
vanished, and Woody was dressed in a gleaming
suit of armor, seated atop a huge stallion.
"I look pretty cool!" he exclaimed.

"But this armor is awfully hot," said Woody after
he had trotted along in the blazing sunshine for
a few minutes. "And it sure is heavy!" he added
a minute later.

"Hey, there's another knight," said Woody. "I
think he wants to joust. No, thank you!" Woody
called as loudly as he could.

CRASH!
"I don't think he heard me," muttered Woody.
"This time I'm going to wish for something peaceful!"

"I know," said Woody, plucking some more
dandelions. "I wish I were the captain of a big
old sailing ship!" And he blew.

"That's more like it," said Woody as he scanned
the calm sea from the deck of his ship.
It was a beautiful evening, with the sun setting
on the horizon.

"Ship ahoy!" shouted a pig from the crow's nest.

Woody turned to look. Another ship was
overtaking them, and it was flying a pirate flag.

The pirate ship came alongside, and the pirates began to hop aboard.

They herded Woody and his crew onto the
foredeck while one of the pirates hung a board
over the water.

"Captain first!" cried the head pirate, poking Woody with his sword. They were going to make him walk the plank! "Now, where did I put that dandelion?" Woody asked himself.

"Ah, there it is, in my buttonhole!" cried Woody
as he somersaulted toward the water. He gave
a great big puff . . .

and was back in his field. Along came his mother.
"Have you been here all afternoon?" she asked.
"Couldn't you think of anything exciting to do?"
Woody just smiled.